The Case of the Mystery Ghost

Book created by Parker C. Hinter

Written by Della Rowland

Illustrated by Chuck Slack

Based on characters from the Parker Brothers game

A Creative Media Applications Production

SCHOLASTIC INC.
New York Toronto London Auckland Sydney

ISBN 0-590-86633-8

12 11 10 9 8 7 6 5 4   8 9/9 0 1/0

Printed in the U.S.A.   40

First Scholastic printing, October 1996

Contents

Look for these Clue™ Jr. books!

The Case of the Secret Message

The Case of the Stolen Jewel

The Case of the Chocolate Fingerprints

The Case of the Missing Movie

The Case of the Zoo Clue

The Case of the Runaway Turtle

Introduction

Meet the members of the Clue Club.

Samantha Scarlet, Peter Plum, Georgie Green, Wendy White, Mortimer Mustard, and Polly Peacock.

These young detectives are all in the same fourth-grade class. The thing they have most in common, though, is their love of mysteries. They formed the Clue Club to talk about mystery books they have read, mystery TV shows and movies they like to watch, and also, to play their favorite game, Clue Jr.

These mystery fans are pretty sharp when it comes to solving real-life mysteries, too. They all use their wits and deductive skills to crack the cases in this book.

You can match *your* wits with this gang of junior detectives to solve the eight mysteries. Can you guess who did it? Check the solution that appears upside down after each story to see if you were right!

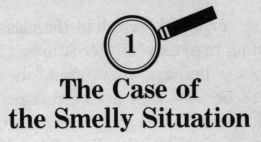

The Case of the Smelly Situation

"**R**emember," Ms. Redding told her fourth-grade class as the dismissal bell rang. "Tomorrow your animal reports are due."

"At least the first report is a cool one," Georgie Green said to the other Clue Jr. Club kids. This was their first big assignment of the year. Ms. Redding had asked the class to do reports on animals that might be found in their backyards. The topics included birds, squirrels, raccoons, possums, rabbits, and skunks. Their reports were supposed to contain information from books as well as personal experiences.

The next morning, Georgie wanted to be the first to give his report. It was on possums. "I saw a possum one night," he said. "When it saw me, it ran under the grate of a sewer drain." He told the class that possums are very shy creatures. "They don't see humans very often," he said. "That's because they are nocturnal."

"Does anyone know what nocturnal means?" asked Ms. Redding. Peter Plum's hand shot up.

"It means they sleep during the day and are active during the night," Peter said.

"That's right, Peter," said Ms. Redding. "Many backyard animals are nocturnal. That means if you see any of them during the day, you should never go near them, because they might be sick with rabies."

Samantha Scarlet told how a skunk in her backyard sprayed her cat, Mittens. "Mittens was standing on the back porch," she explained to the class. "The skunk was coming toward the house when it saw Mittens. All of a sudden it turned around and lifted its tail. That's when it sprayed my cat. We had to give her a bath in tomato juice. Boy, was she mad."

"How far away from your cat was the

skunk, Samantha?" asked Ms. Redding.

"About ten feet," Samantha said. "After Mittens got sprayed, I looked up skunks in the encyclopedia. I found out they can spray something that is twelve feet away and hit it like a bull's-eye."

"Sounds like skunks are good animals to avoid," said Ms. Redding.

"Oh, they're not so bad," said Samantha. "You're pretty safe as long as they're facing you or their tails are down. They have to lift their tails to spray."

Mortimer Mustard gave a report on squirrels and how some got into his attic one winter. Polly Peacock's report was on raccoons. She talked about the family of raccoons who lived in a hollow tree stump in the wooded lot behind her house. Wendy White did her report on the hummingbirds that came every day to the special feeder she made for them.

Then the bell rang. School was over for the week.

"We'll have to finish the rest of our reports on Monday," said Ms. Redding. "I have to admit, I'm looking forward to them. You've all done excellent jobs, especially on the personal stories. Have a nice weekend."

Outside in the school yard, Wendy asked Peter what animal he chose. "I'm doing my report on moles," said Peter. "They aren't very popular backyard animals, so I thought I'd see why."

"What did you find out?" asked Polly.

"Moles dig tunnels in the ground that ruin the lawn," said Peter. "But that's not the only reason I wanted to do moles. My next-door neighbor, Mr. Wallace, set up a mole trap in his backyard last week. He catches them and lets them go in the woods. I was hoping he would catch one so I could study it for my report, but he hasn't yet."

"The weekly Clue Jr. Club meeting is at your house tomorrow," said Mortimer. "Can we look at Mr. Wallace's trap then?"

"Sure," said Peter. "I know he won't mind."

The next day, when everyone arrived at Peter's house, he was too excited to start the meeting. "Mr. Wallace caught something in his mole trap," he told the others. "But it isn't a mole. It's a skunk!"

"Oh, no!" exclaimed Samantha. "What's he going to do?"

"It's a problem," said Peter. "He wants to let it out in the woods, but he's afraid he'll get sprayed if he gets too close to the trap."

"Does the skunk look sick?" asked Georgie.

"No. It's fine," said Peter. "It got caught in the trap last night when it was wandering around the neighborhood."

"It's nocturnal," Georgie reminded everyone. "That means it —"

"We remember, Georgie," said Polly. "Thank you."

"Can we see it?" asked Wendy.

The kids went out in Peter's backyard to look at the skunk next door. A group of police officers had arrived. They were standing around talking about what they should do with the animal.

"The cage isn't very big, is it?" said Mortimer. "The skunk barely fits in it."

"Watch out, kids," said Officer Lawford. "We don't want anyone to get sprayed."

"What are you going to do?" asked Mortimer.

"I'm not sure yet," said Officer Lawford. "But this is a big problem."

"I don't think this is a big problem," said Samantha. "I know how to save the skunk." She walked across Mr. Wallace's yard straight toward the skunk.

"Stop!" cried Polly. "You will get sprayed."

"No, I won't," said Samantha.

"Watch out, Samantha," said Officer Lawford. "The skunk's spray could hurt

your eyes if it hits you in the face."

"It won't spray me," Samantha told him, walking over to the cage. "Look."

Why is Samantha so sure the skunk won't spray her?

Solution
The Case of the Smelly Situation

Sure enough, nothing happened when Samantha reached the cage. The skunk just looked up at her curiously. "Do you have an old towel, Mr. Wallace?" she asked.

"Well, I'll be," Mr. Wallace said. "I'll be right back." He went into his house and came back with a towel. Samantha threw it over the cage.

"Now you can take the skunk back to the woods, Mr. Wallace," said Samantha. "Just get out of the way quickly after you open the cage."

The police helped Mr. Wallace put the skunk in the back of his car. Afterward, Officer Lawford came over to Samantha. "How did you know the skunk wouldn't spray you?" he asked.

"Because the cage was too small for the skunk, so its tail was caught," said Samantha.

"I get it," said Peter. "The skunk couldn't raise its tail."

"I remember," said Mortimer. "They have to raise their tails to spray."

"Well, I'm impressed, Samantha," said Officer Lawford.

"Me too," laughed Georgie. "This case could have been a real stinker."

The Case of
the Mystery Ghost

It was a cool, brisk October evening. The full moon lit up the streets as the Clue Jr. Club kids made their way to the outskirts of town. They were headed for the Simpson Manor, a deserted mansion that sat at the top of a hill. All the kids in town said the house was haunted and that a ghost lived on the second floor. Every so often some kids tried to stay in the house, but so far no one had lasted longer than half an hour.

Richie Royal, the town bully, had bet the Clue Jr. Club kids a pizza that they couldn't stay in the house for one hour. When the kids accepted the bet, they didn't give it much thought. Now that they were actually going to the house, they were a little scared.

After they arrived, the kids walked

around a bit before going inside. Georgie Green was about to go in through the back door when Wendy White yelled, "Look out, Georgie!"

"Aaah!" screamed Georgie, running back to the group. "Do you see a ghost, Wendy?"

"No," she answered. "But look what you were about to walk through." She pointed to a huge spiderweb across the door.

"Wow!" exclaimed Peter Plum. "It would have been a shame to ruin such a magnificent web."

"We better go around to the front door," Wendy said.

Just then, Mortimer Mustard saw something flash by one of the side windows. "Look!" he cried. "The ghost!"

"I didn't see anything," said Polly Peacock.

"Why did we make that bet with Richie?" complained Samantha Scarlet, shivering. "He probably won't pay up even if we win."

"We might as well go inside," quaked Mortimer, "and get it over with."

The kids walked slowly up the stairs. They stood on the second-floor landing for a few minutes.

"Well, I guess we should go in the rooms," said Georgie. No one moved. "You first, Peter," Georgie said.

"Ah . . . okay," stammered Peter. "Come on, guys." He led the way into one of the front rooms. Inside was some furniture covered with sheets. "Let's check out another room," Peter said.

After looking in several rooms in the house, Mortimer piped up. "Hey, this isn't so bad."

"Maybe this ghost thing is just a hoot!" laughed Georgie.

"Oooooooh!" The kids heard a low moan.

"What's that?" whispered Polly.

"It's just the wind," said Samantha. "Calm down, Polly."

"OOOOOOOOH!" went the voice again, only louder.

"That's not the wind," said Peter. "It sounds sort of like a person."

At that, some of the outside shutters on the second floor began banging.

"You're right, Peter! That's not the wind!" shouted Samantha.

"It's the ghost!" shrieked Mortimer.

"Let's get out of here!" cried Polly.

The kids ran down the stairs. Then, through the open front door they saw Richie Royal running across the yard.

"It's only Richie," said Peter.

"Yeah, and he's trying to scare us," fumed Samantha.

"Richie!" Georgie shouted from the doorway. "We see you! Come back!" Richie turned when he heard them calling and loped back up to the house.

"What are you doing here, Richie?" asked Polly.

"Making sure you stuck around. What do you think?" muttered Richie. "I wanted to protect my bet."

"I think you were pretending to be a ghost," said Wendy. "You were trying to scare us so we'd lose the bet."

"Not me," said Richie sincerely. "In fact, I heard the ghost myself. That's why I was running away."

"You heard it?" exclaimed Mortimer, looking over his shoulder.

"Sure," Richie said. "It was moaning something awful. I could hear it all the way downstairs. Boy, when it started banging those shutters, I couldn't take it anymore. I made a run for it out the back door. I don't care about our bet anymore. Honest. In fact, I think we better get out of here now before the ghost gets us."

"You mean before the hour is up, don't you?" said Peter.

"I'm not kidding," Richie said. "I'm scared! Let's get out of here." He headed out the front door and down the porch steps.

"You're lying, Richie," said Peter. "You're the ghost."

How can Peter prove that Richie was the culprit?

Solution
The Case of the Mystery Ghost

"Okay, Mr. Mystery Man," snarled Richie. "Prove it."

"Well, I'll bet that you're lying about running through the back door," Peter said.

"You're on!" said Richie. "How do you know I didn't run through the back door? You were upstairs."

"Because you couldn't have gone through the back door," laughed Samantha.

"What are you talking about?" shouted Richie.

"Come this way, Richie," said Polly. "We'll show you." Everyone walked to the back of the house. "See?" she said, pointing at the back door. "That's how I knew you couldn't have gone through."

Across the door hung the huge spider-web.

"If you had run through the back door, you would have torn the web down, and you would have shreds of it on your clothes," said Wendy. "But it's still perfect."

"Looks like I win the bet about you running through the back door," said Peter. "Now I'll bet you there's a ladder against the house." Sure enough, when the kids walked around the side of the house, the ladder was there near the shutters. Caught in several lies, Richie confessed to pretending to be the ghost.

"But the pizza you'll buy us will be the real thing," said Samantha.

"Richie was caught in his own web of lies," laughed Georgie.

The Case of the Winning Ticket

Thanksgiving was around the corner, and the community center was having a food-and-clothing drive for charity. The Clue Jr. Club kids decided to bring in canned goods and some clothes they had outgrown.

When they arrived, they saw that the community center had also set up several booths to raise money. Mortimer Mustard spotted a bakery booth right away.

"Let's see what kind of pies they're selling," he told the others.

"First let's get our tickets for the raffle," said Polly Peacock. "The winner gets one quarter of the money in the pot."

"And the second prize is two pumpkin pies, Mortimer," laughed Samantha.

"Hey!" said Mortimer. "I hope I come in second."

Two high school students, Carl Claret and Marla Maroon, were running the raffle. Each wore a tag that read TEENS FOR THANKSGIVING RAFFLE pinned to his or her jacket with a large safety pin.

"That's one big safety pin," said Georgie Green, pointing to Marla's tag.

"Your tag is crooked," Polly told Carl.

"Oh, okay," he said, and reached up to adjust it.

Carl pointed to the roll of raffle tickets. "So. You want to buy a ticket or not?"

"Not just yet," said Wendy. "I want the last one. It's the luckiest number."

"Not me," said Marla. "I want the first one. *That's* the lucky one. In fact, here's my dollar now, Carl." Marla gave Carl a dollar and he handed her a ticket. The ticket had a number on each end and a dotted line down the middle. Each contestant was supposed to rip the ticket in two, put one half in the ticket bowl, and keep the other half to prove whose ticket it was. Marla put it into her pocket.

"Aren't you going to put it into the bowl?" asked Polly.

"Not yet," said Marla. She closed her eyes and put her fingers on her forehead. "Now isn't the right time. I can feel it."

"We're not set up yet, anyway," said Carl. "It wouldn't be fair."

A half hour later, the kids were at the photo booth getting a group shot taken. The photographer was adjusting a light behind them when she tripped over a cord and stepped on the drop curtain. *RIIIIPPPPPP.*

"Oh, no," said the photographer. "I don't have anything to mend this with."

"A safety pin would do the trick," said her assistant.

"Hey, Carl and Marla have safety pins," remembered Mortimer. "Big ones."

"One of them would be perfect," exclaimed Wendy. "Let's see if they'll give it to the photo booth."

"I don't have mine anymore," Marla told the kids when they asked her for a pin.

"Mrs. Wilson at the baked goods table needed it to hold up the sign over the booth, so I gave it to her."

"I don't know what happened to mine," said Carl. "I took my tag off after it ripped and put it down somewhere."

"Oh, too bad," said Peter. "Oh, well, too many people need safety pins today."

"Speaking of baked goods, let's lend some support to that booth," said Mortimer.

The kids had a hard time finding the bakery booth because it had no sign.

"That's odd," said Peter when they finally found the booth. "Didn't Marla say she gave her safety pin to Mrs. Wilson to hold up her sign?"

"Yeah, she did," said Samantha. "But Mrs. Wilson doesn't even have a sign."

"Maybe she hasn't put it back up yet," said Wendy. "She looks pretty busy."

"Where's your sign, Mrs. Wilson?" asked Georgie.

"Never had time to make one," said Mrs. Wilson cheerfully. "But it hasn't seemed to hurt us. We're almost out of cranberry pie."

"Cranberry pie!" exclaimed Mortimer. "Oh, I've never had that kind of pie. I'll have a slice of that, please."

The kids walked around to the rest of the booths. Soon it was time for the drawing. "I'd better get back and buy my ticket," said Wendy.

When Wendy bought her ticket, Carl said, "Just in time, Wendy. I was going to announce the last chance to buy raffle tickets." Carl plunged both of his hands into the tickets and began stirring them. "This is to make sure the drawing is fair," he told everyone watching.

"Hurry up, Carl," said Samantha. "The suspense is killing me."

Finally, Carl pulled out a ticket. "Here's the winner," he shouted. "Number one three five five three."

"That's mine!" Marla exclaimed. "See, Wendy. I told you the first ticket was lucky."

Wendy looked at her ticket number. It was 13353. "My number is very similar to the one you called out," she told Carl. "Can I look at the ticket to make sure you didn't misread it?"

"Oh sure," said Carl. "We want to be fair."

The kids inspected the winning ticket closely. "What's that third number?" asked Georgie. "I can't read it. There are holes in the ticket."

"It's a five," said Wendy sadly. "Marla's the winner, all right."

"Maybe you'll win the pies, Wendy," Mortimer told her.

Meanwhile, Carl had both arms in the ticket bowl again, sifting through the stubs. He waited until he had everyone's attention before he pulled out another ticket. "And here is the second prize," he shouted. He handed the ticket to Wendy.

"Here, Wendy, why don't you read the number?"

The Clue Club gathered around Wendy to check out the number. "There are holes in this ticket, too," she said. "But I can read the numbers."

When she called out the numbers, another friend of Carl's claimed the second prize.

"Your friends are lucky today," Mrs. Givemore, the head of the Community Center, said to Carl.

"Something is fishy," whispered Polly. "But how to prove it?"

"I agree," said Samantha. "But how could Carl pick the two tickets he wanted?"

Carl overheard the Clue Club talking about him fixing the drawing. "Hey, you little creeps, are you trying to pin something on me?"

"That's it!" says Peter. He stepped up to the raffle booth. "Carl, I'll help you clean up your booth."

"Swell," said Carl.

"Give me the raffle-ticket bowl," said Peter. "I'll empty it."

"No!" yelled Carl. "I mean, not yet. We may need to draw for a third prize or something."

"You think you can win the third prize, too, Carl?" said Peter. "You couldn't have won the first two without some help."

"What are you talking about?" Carl said.

"You rigged the drawing," said Peter.

"Can you prove that, Peter?" asked Mrs. Givemore.

"Yes, by cleaning up your booth," Peter said to Carl.

How does Peter know Carl and Marla rigged the drawing?

"Or safety pins in the bowl," said Mortimer.

"I think we'll have another drawing," said Mrs. Givemore. "And this time someone else will draw."

"And this time the drawing *will* be fair," said Georgie.

Solution
The Case of the Winning Ticket

Peter emptied the raffle-ticket bowl. Among the tickets were two large safety pins.

"Here they are," Peter said, picking up the pins. He slid a pin through the two holes in each of the winning tickets.

"I see," said Wendy. "Carl and Marla put the safety pins on their raffle tickets. Then when Carl sifted through the tickets, he could feel for the tickets with safety pins."

"All he had to do was remove the pins before he took the tickets out of the bowl," said Samantha.

"That's why it took him so long to pull out each ticket," said Peter. "First he had to find a ticket with a safety pin through it, then he had to take the pin off the ticket."

"No one would notice two little holes in the tickets," said Polly.

The Case of the Candy Cane Culprit

"**P**eter, you guys have got to help me!" Georgie Green wailed into the phone.

Peter Plum held the phone away from his ear. "Calm down, pal," he said. "What can be so terrible? There's no school for a week. It's snowing, so you can go sledding. There are Christmas presents under your tree. Why are you having such a bad time? What's the problem?"

"It's a mystery, that's what it is," Georgie said. "Candy canes keep disappearing from our Christmas tree." Georgie explained that his mother was accusing him or Bingo, his pet monkey, of taking the candy canes.

"You have to come over," Georgie said.

"All right," said Peter. "I'll call the others and we'll be right over."

When the Clue Jr. Club kids arrived at Georgie's house, he described what had been going on. "Every day some candy canes disappear from the tree," he said. "At first, Mom just put more on, but now she says it's getting out of hand. She thinks it's me, but it's not."

"What about Bingo?" said Polly Peacock.

"Well, he does like sweets," said Georgie. "But I never give him much. It's not good for him."

"Then what's this?" said Mortimer Mustard, pointing to a candy cane wrapper in Bingo's cage.

"I didn't notice that there," Georgie exclaimed. He shook his finger at Bingo. "It sure looks like you're the candy cane culprit, Bingo," he said.

"Let's let him out of his cage and see if he takes any candy off the tree," suggested Wendy.

The kids watched the little monkey all afternoon, trying to catch him in the act.

But Bingo didn't go near the canes on the tree.

Around three o'clock, Mrs. Green came into the living room. "Could you kids do me a favor?" she said. "It's finally stopped snowing and I wonder if you would shovel the walk before Mr. Green gets home."

"Sure, Mom," said Georgie. The kids put on their coats and boots and grabbed shovels and brooms.

"Look!" laughed Wendy. "Bingo is ready to help." Bingo had put on Mr. Green's hunting hat and was waiting near the door holding his toy shovel.

"My dad always wears that hat when he shovels snow," Georgie told the others. "Bingo must be imitating him."

Outside, Bingo shoveled a little snow. Then he took off the hunting hat and looked into it. After a minute, he dumped a bunch of cellophane candy cane wrappers out of the hat — all over the clean sidewalk.

"So, Bingo, this is what you've been doing with most of your empty wrappers," scolded Georgie. "You've been hiding them in Dad's hat."

The kids picked up the wrappers and finished shoveling. Meanwhile, Bingo found an unopened candy cane in the hat. He held it up for Georgie to see.

"I guess you can have that one," said Georgie. "It's broken and Mom would just throw it away anyway."

Mr. Green arrived home while the kids were having some hot cocoa at the dining room table. "Hi, kids," he said. "I hear you've already shoveled the front walk. I appreciate that. It was real hectic at work today."

"We'll finish the back as soon as we warm up," said Samantha.

Mr. Green put on his coat and hunting hat. "That's okay," he told them. "I'd actually like to finish the back walk. I could use some exercise after sitting all day."

Just as the kids were finishing up their cocoa, Mrs. Green came in and told them more candy canes were missing. "Bingo's

done it again," she said. She pointed underneath the table where Bingo was sitting.

The kids looked under the table. After a moment, Mortimer said, "You know, Bingo might not be the one we're looking for."

"Well, it sure isn't me," said Georgie. "You guys are my witnesses. I haven't been near the tree since we came in from shoveling."

"No, it isn't you or Bingo," said Mortimer. "To tell you the truth, I think it might be . . . your dad!"

Why does Mortimer think the candy cane thief is Mr. Green?

backyard and asked him to take off his hat. Inside were three empty cellophane wrappers and two more unopened candy canes. Red-faced, Mr. Green admitted he'd been taking the canes off the tree.

"I love peppermint," he said.

"I'd say you kids pulled this case out of the hat," laughed Mrs. Green.

Solution
The Case of the Candy Cane Culprit

"What?" cried Mrs. Green.

"Whoever heard of a grown-up stealing candy canes?" Georgie giggled.

"Well, look at Bingo's candy cane," Mortimer said. "It's the same one he found in the hat."

"How can you tell?" asked Samantha.

"Because it's broken the same way," explained Mortimer. "It looks like he isn't very interested in the candy."

"You're right, Mortimer," said Wendy.

"Bingo hasn't even opened it, let alone eaten it."

"He isn't even playing with it," said Polly.

"And don't forget the candy cane wrappers he found in Mr. Green's hat," said Peter.

"Which means Mr. Green could be the culprit," finished Polly.

Mrs. Green called Mr. Green in from the

5

The Case of the False Claim

At the end of their weekly Clue Jr. Club meeting, Peter Plum brought up some new business. "A mystery movie, *Riddle of the Pyramids*, just opened at the big movie theater in the new mall," he told his friends.

"Oooh," sighed Samantha Scarlet. "It's supposed to be great. But how can we get to the mall?"

"My dad said he'd give us a ride there and back this afternoon if we wanted to go," said Peter. "He and my mom want to do some clothes shopping at the new stores."

"I have to call my folks," said Mortimer Mustard.

"Me too," said Polly Peacock. "Mom

wanted to change my violin lesson to Monday, but I better make sure she did."

By the time the Clue Club finished lunch, everything was arranged. The kids piled into the Plums' van and were off to the two o'clock showing of *Riddle of the Pyramids*.

They arrived a little early so, after the kids bought their tickets, they walked around the new mall. Right next to the theater was a candy-and-sandwich shop.

"Hmmm," said Mortimer. "Think we have time to buy a bag of Chock-Os?"

"Sure," said Samantha. "We won't be at the movie concession stand for at least fifteen minutes." Everyone laughed because Mortimer was always hungry.

"Funny." Mortimer sniffed. "I guess that means you wouldn't want one."

"Oh, I take it back, Mortimer!" laughed Samantha. "I want some chocolate."

A boy who was ahead of them in line bought a can of soda. They watched as he stuffed it into the front pocket of his sweat-shirt.

"I'll bet he's going to take his soda into the theater," whispered Polly.

"But that's against the rules," said Wendy White.

"True," said Georgie Green. "But the food at these theaters is so expensive that a lot of kids do it anyway."

"The newspaper had an article on the new mall. It said this new theater has a way to stop kids from doing that," said Peter. "There's a buzzer that people who work there press when they see someone sneaking in with food. The buzzer rings in the guard's room. When he hears it, he comes out and takes the food away."

"Wow," said Georgie. "They're pretty serious about this."

"Yeah," agreed Peter. "The article said that movie theaters make a lot of money on food and drinks. I guess it's worth it to them."

"Oh well," said Samantha. "I don't have

to worry about getting caught. I'm going to buy some nice hot popcorn in the theater."

"Me too," said Mortimer, as he finished the last piece of chocolate. "With lots of butter."

The boy with the soda in his pocket walked through the front door of the movie theater just ahead of the kids. He headed straight for *Riddle of the Pyramids*.

"Hey! The boy with the soda is going to the mystery movie, too," said Peter.

"Let's see if he gets caught with his soda," said Wendy.

"First, let's get our food," said Mortimer. The kids walked over to the concession stand. "The line's not moving yet," he reported to the rest of his friends.

The kids made it to the movie line just as the boy was ready to enter the door. As the boy gave his ticket to the ticket taker by the theater door, a guard came up to him.

"See?" whispered Peter excitedly. "I told you he'd get caught."

"What's the problem here?" the guard asked the boy.

"No problem," the boy said.

"Looks like you got something there," said the guard, patting the kid's bulging front sweatshirt pocket. "You have to turn over that soda. No food or drinks allowed from the outside."

The boy reached into his sweatshirt pocket and pulled out the soda can.

The guard turned to the ticket taker. "Did you ring the buzzer?" he asked.

"Yeah," the ticket taker answered. "My name is Tab Tan."

"Okay, Tab," said the guard. "I'll put that in my report. The reward will show up in your paycheck."

Just then a girl came running up. "I'm Cindy Cinnamon. I work at the concession stand," she told the guard. "I saw this kid going into the mystery movie with a soda in his sweatshirt pocket so I rang the alarm."

"Wait a minute," said the guard. "Tab

just said *he* pushed the alarm. Now you say you did. Which one of you is telling the truth?"

"Can't you tell which buzzer was pushed?" Peter asked the guard.

"No," he answered. "The system can't tell which buzzer it was. It only tells me which movie to go to." He shook his head. "I knew this would happen when they told me there's no way to tell exactly who rings the buzzer."

The guard turned to Tab and Cindy. "Well, only one of you is telling the truth. Which one is it?"

"You know what?" said Georgie. "I think I know who pushed the alarm."

How does Georgie know who pushed the alarm?

Solution
The Case of the False Claim

"Well, speak up, kid," the guard said to Georgie.

"It was Tab," Georgie answered. Turning to Cindy, he said, "You couldn't have seen the soda can."

"Why not?" said Cindy.

"Because you only saw the back of the boy," explained Georgie.

"That's right," said Peter. "The soda can was in his front pocket."

"I saw him come in the front door," said Cindy.

"You couldn't have," said Samantha. "The concession stand faces the other way."

"You must have been walking by just now and saw him pull the soda can out of his sweatshirt," said Polly.

"Then you decided to take the credit for catching him," said Mortimer.

"And the reward," said Wendy.

"Let's go see if they're right," the guard

said to Cindy. He walked into the concession stand. "You're right, kids," he told
them. "I can't see the front doors or the
movie door from here, Cindy, it looks like
you got caught, too."

The guard turned to the Clue Jr. Club
kids. "Good work, guys," he told them.
"The theater should give you a job here
catching liars."

"We'd be happy if they just gave us some
free food," said Mortimer as everyone
laughed.

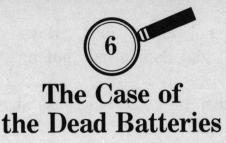

The Case of
the Dead Batteries

The fourth grade was putting on a talent show and the students had been practicing after school all week. Polly Peacock was playing a violin piece. Peter Plum and Georgie Green were giving a karate demonstration. Mortimer Mustard was going to tell jokes, and Wendy White and Samantha Scarlet were singing a song from a new cartoon movie.

All the fourth-graders were excited about the talent show. Lauren Loden was looking forward to performing her acrobatic act. And Oscar Oatmeal, the class clown, was sure his comedy routine would be the hit of the talent show. Roy Reddy, a new student from Texas, wanted to play guitar and sing some "real Texas songs" for everyone.

"I'm not crazy about Roy's country music," said Samantha, "but he sure can sing."

"I'll bet he could sing just about anything," said Wendy.

"Singing's not everything," said Oscar, frowning.

"Of course not, Oscar," said Ken Copper, holding out five colored wooden balls. "There's juggling. Wait till you catch my act. Get it? *Catch* my act?"

"Oooh," groaned Polly. "I'm laughing so hard I can't catch my breath."

Just then, Ms. Brightman, the drama teacher, called everyone to rehearsal. She put her boom box on the piano. "Wendy and Samantha, we'll start with your number," she said. When the girls were ready, the teacher pushed the play button on the boom box. Nothing happened. "Oh, no, not again," she groaned.

"It looks like someone is leaving it on all night," she said as she took the batteries out.

"But why would someone do that?" asked Mortimer.

"I have no idea," the teacher said.

"Whatever is happening is holding up my music career," sighed Polly. "We haven't been able to rehearse for two days now. The talent show is the day after tomorrow."

"That leaves only one more day to polish our acts," moaned Lauren. "I'll never be ready."

"Let me see if I can find the cord to the boom box," Ms. Brightman said. She went to her office and returned a moment later, empty-handed.

"Nope," she said. "It must be at home. I'll bring it in tomorrow. Along with some spare batteries."

"I hope we can get the boom box to work for the dress rehearsal tomorrow," said Oscar.

"Oh, I'm sure the boom box is fine, Oscar," Ms. Brightman told him. "The batteries are just run down. And don't worry. You'll be a big hit, I know."

The next day, there was a thunderstorm just after school let out, and the electricity went off for about twenty minutes. As a result, the rehearsal was late getting started.

"Some of the students have gone home," worried Ms. Brightman. "I was hoping everyone could be here for the final run-through."

"I'm here," Oscar called from the front of the auditorium. "I had to walk my little sister home."

"Me too," said Lauren, throwing her coat on top of a seat in the back of the auditorium. She looked down at something in the seat. It was the boom box. "Do you want me to bring your boom box to the stage, Ms. Brightman?" she asked.

"Yes, Lauren. Thank you," said Ms. Brightman. "I was just looking for that in my office. Wonder when I brought it out here?"

"Is it working okay?" asked Samantha.

"I'm sure it is," Ms. Brightman said. She

put some new batteries in and turned the boom box on. "Whoops!" she said as music blasted. She quickly turned down the volume.

"Sounds good." The teacher smiled. "Now let's make sure the batteries are strong enough to play a tape." She opened the tape deck to insert a tape. "Oh, I see there's a tape already in there. We'll just play it." She pressed a button and country music filled the room.

"Hey," Roy said. "That sounds like one of my tapes. Unless someone else in this school likes country music." Everyone laughed.

"No, it's yours," said Oscar, holding his hands over his ears.

"He's right," said Ms. Brightman, holding up the tape. "Here's your name printed on it."

"What was it doing in the boom box?" Roy said.

"Say, I heard that tape playing in the boys' dressing room before I went to take my sister home," said Oscar. "I bet Roy was playing it on the boom box."

"Did you use the boom box this afternoon, Roy?" asked Ms. Brightman.

"No, ma'am," said Roy. "Anyway, I have my own cassette player."

"But you can only hear music through your earphones with your cassette player," said Oscar. "Maybe you wanted to hear the tape louder or something."

"I haven't listened to that tape since this morning when I was walking to school," said Roy.

"Then how come I heard it?" said Oscar.

"Well, all I can say is someone else took my tape and played it in Ms. Brightman's boom box," said Roy.

"Come on," said Oscar. "No one in the school likes country music but you."

"Roy," said Lauren, "are you the one who's been leaving the boom box on all night and running down the batteries?"

"Me?" said Roy. "No way."

"Then how do you explain your country

tape being in the boom box?" said Ms. Brightman.

"Yeah," said Oscar. "Who would do that except you, Roy?"

"I think you did, Oscar," said Polly.

"Me?" said Oscar. "Why me?"

"You gave yourself away," replied Polly.

How does Polly know Oscar is the one using the boom box?

Solution
The Case of the Dead Batteries

"Because you couldn't have heard Roy's tape playing after school," said Polly.

"What do you mean?" said Oscar.

"Ms. Brightman took the old batteries out last night," said Peter. "So there were no batteries in the boom box."

"I know that," said Oscar. "Roy didn't need batteries. He used the cord. See? The cord is right there on the radio."

"Wrong again," said Mortimer. "The storm after school knocked out the electricity until just a little while ago."

"You didn't know that because you weren't here," said Wendy.

"I don't get it. Why did you run down the batteries, Oscar?" asked Georgie.

"So no one would be able to practice the next day," Oscar explained. "I wanted my act to be the best. And I knew Roy would get blamed if I put his tape in the boom box. Then maybe he'd be disqualified from the show."

"Sounds like you're jealous of Roy," said Ms. Brightman.

"I just didn't want him to be better than me in the talent show," Oscar said.

"This isn't a competition, Oscar," said Ms. Brightman. "This show is a time for each of you to show off your own special talent. Roy may sing well, but you know how to make people laugh."

"You sure won't win any awards for this performance, Oscar," said Georgie.

58

The Case of
the Stolen Mirror

"**W**e've got a case," Peter Plum told Georgie Green on the phone. "Call Mortimer and Polly and I'll call Samantha and Wendy. We'll all meet at Nancy Nutmeg's house in half an hour."

When the Clue Jr. Club kids arrived at Nancy's, she was standing in her driveway waiting for them.

"What happened, Nancy?" asked Peter.

"This is the scene of the crime," Nancy told them.

"Okay. We'll check for clues as soon as you tell us what happened," said Wendy White.

"See this hatbox?" Nancy asked, pointing to an old decorated hatbox sitting in the driveway next to her. "My dad bought it for my mom today at a flea market. It's my mom's birthday this Sunday."

"Yeah, yeah," said Mortimer Mustard impatiently. "What does that have to do with the crime?"

"Everything!" said Nancy. "Dad was going to put flowers in the box and give them to Mom. Anyway, he decided to keep the box in the garage until Sunday so she wouldn't see it. But he took the hatbox out of the trunk of his car before he pulled the car into the garage. Then he came into the house to get me."

"Why?" asked Georgie. "Couldn't he carry a hatbox by himself?"

"Of course, silly," said Nancy. "He came to tell me that he had a surprise for me in the box."

"Oh! What did he get you?" asked Polly Peacock.

"An antique hand mirror," Nancy answered. "He put it inside the hatbox after he parked the car."

"Can we see it?" asked Samantha Scarlet.

"No," said Nancy. "And that's why I called you guys."

"You called us because we can't see the mirror," said Georgie. "This case is very confusing."

"No, it's not," said Nancy. "When my dad and I got outside and opened the hatbox, the mirror was gone. That's why I called you. Any ideas, guys?"

"How long was your father inside the house?" asked Wendy.

"Like thirty seconds," said Nancy.

"Well then it had to be someone who was close," said Polly.

"Let's check with the neighbors to see if they saw anything," suggested Peter.

"Good idea, Peter," said Georgie. The Clue Jr. Club kids waited outside while Nancy called up her two neighbors and asked them to come over.

Carole Creme, who lived on one side, said she heard the car trunk slam shut.

"But I didn't pay any attention," she said. "I was brushing my cat. I didn't even look out the window to see what Mr. Nutmeg was taking out of the trunk."

Harry Hunter lived on the other side of Nancy. "I didn't hear anything," he said. "But I did see Patrick Periwinkle walk by about that time. He could have taken the mirror."

"Should we go ask Patrick?" asked Nancy.

"I don't think so," said Wendy. "Carole took the mirror."

"But I told you, I didn't even look outside," Carole protested.

"And that was your mistake," said Wendy.

Why does Wendy think Carole took the mirror?

Solution
The Case of the Stolen Mirror

"For one thing, you knew that it was the trunk that slammed," Wendy told Carole.

"Yeah," said Peter. "How did she know it was the trunk and not the car door slamming if she didn't look outside?"

"And how did she know Mr. Nutmeg took something out?" said Samantha. "He could have just put something in."

"Yes," said Wendy. "And she saw Mr. Nutmeg take the hatbox out of the trunk, pull the car into the garage, put the mirror in the box, and go into the house."

"And she saw the hatbox in the drive-way," finished Georgie.

"Okay. I took the mirror," Carole confessed. "This is no excuse, but I didn't have a Mother's Day present for my mom. I'm sorry, Nancy. I'll go get it for you."

"I guess we slammed the door shut on this case," said Georgie.

The Case of
the Broken Golf Club

After their weekly Clue Club meeting, the Clue kids were discussing how to find summer jobs.

"I'm baby-sitting for the Kinzlers," said Wendy White. "But it's only once a week."

"I'm going to weed Mrs. Lavender's garden," said Polly Peacock. "But I won't make much."

"Before school let out, I asked Mr. Higgins if he knew of any jobs," said Georgie Green.

"Good idea. A school principal should know these things," said Mortimer Mustard. "What did he say?"

"He said we were probably too young for most jobs," shrugged Georgie.

"Sammy Stripe told me he was working

at the golf course this summer," said Samantha Scarlet. "He's our age."

"That reminds me," Peter Plum said. "Robbie Russet got a job there, too! Can you believe it?" Robbie was an eighth-grader who was known for being lazy.

"You're kidding," said Polly. "What is he doing?"

"Watering the grass," snickered Peter.

Polly rolled her eyes.

"Geez," moaned Mortimer. "Robbie has all the luck."

"Yeah," agreed Samantha. "Leave it to the laziest kid in town to get the easiest job."

"You're all just jealous," said Wendy, laughing.

"You're right, I am," said Georgie. "I'd love to have a job at the golf course. I bet they'd let you hit a few balls in your spare time."

"Or maybe caddie," said Mortimer.

"We should go see if there are any more

jobs there," said Peter. "If Sammy and Robbie can work there, maybe we can, too."

That afternoon, the kids biked over to the golf course clubhouse to talk to the manager, Mr. Tee. "Sure, we pay kids your age to hunt lost golf balls on the green once a week," he told them. "But right now, I have a list as long as my arm of kids who want that job. Tell you what, though. I'll take your names and numbers. I admire kids who want to work."

On their way out, the kids asked Mr. Tee where Sammy was.

"Sammy's on the third green," he replied. "He'll be coming back in soon, if you want to wait out front."

The kids walked outside. A hose with a sprinkler attachment was lying on the grass in front of the clubhouse.

"Looks like Robbie is hard at work," giggled Wendy, pointing to the hose. Just then, a big fancy car pulled up into the clubhouse driveway. The car's tire stopped right on the hose that was watering the grass.

"Hey!" Georgie called to the driver. "Your car is sitting on the hose."

"The tire is stopping the water from flowing through," worried Polly. "Won't the hose break?"

"It's okay," the driver laughed. "Those hoses are strong. Besides, I'll only be a few minutes."

"Hi, guys! What are you doing here?" called a voice behind them. The kids turned around to see Sammy Stripe heading toward them. He was carrying a bag of golf clubs.

"We came to see if we could get jobs," Peter said.

"Cool! I'll put in a good word for you with the manager," said Sammy. "Listen. I'll be finished in about fifteen minutes. Wait for me."

"Fifteen minutes?" said Mortimer. He

looked worried. "How about if we get something to eat in the clubhouse?" he asked the others. "I'm starving."

"Of course, Mortimer," laughed Samantha. "It *has* been half an hour since we had lunch."

"We'll meet you here, Sammy," said Wendy.

Fifteen minutes later, the kids met Sammy in front of the clubhouse. They were about to leave when the driver of the parked car stormed out of the clubhouse. He got into his car, slammed the door shut, and drove away.

"That was a long few minutes," said Polly, looking at her watch.

"Wonder why he was so mad?" said Sammy.

"Look, there's Robbie," said Peter, pointing to Robbie coming from behind the clubhouse.

"Hey, Robbie," everyone called out.

"Hey," Robbie said as he turned off the water faucet. "What are you doing here?"

"We came to see if there were any more cushy jobs like yours," laughed Samantha.

"Very funny," said Robbie. "I'll have you know it's hard work carrying these heavy hoses around, standing in the hot sun hour after hour. . . ."

"Okay, okay," said Polly. "We get the picture."

"Face it, guys," Robbie bragged. "I have all the luck. You have none."

Just then, Mr. Tee came out of the clubhouse carrying a set of golf clubs. He seemed upset. "You didn't borrow these clubs today, did you, son?" he asked Robbie.

"No, sir," Robbie answered. "Say, didn't you just come in with a bag of clubs, Sammy?"

"Yeah," Sammy said. "But they were Mr. Overdone's. I was caddying for him."

"You didn't try these out after you came in, Sammy?" Mr. Tee asked.

"Not me," said Sammy. "I wouldn't use a member's clubs."

"Did either of you notice anyone using them this afternoon?" he asked.

"Mr. Archwell used them earlier," said Sammy. "I caddied for him. But I thought they belonged to him."

"They do!" Mr. Tee sighed. "But someone else used them later, and broke one of the clubs. Mr. Archwell was just here to pick them up and he was furious. He had left them while he went to an appointment in town. When he came to pick them up, we discovered one club was broken."

"Well, I didn't see anyone else using them," said Robbie. "But I've been out here watering the front grass. I gave it a real good soak, just like you asked me to."

"We'll pay Mr. Archwell for his broken club," said Mr. Tee. "But it's not just the money. Our members have to trust the golf staff to take care of their equipment or they'll cancel their memberships."

"Excuse me, sir," said Wendy. "I'm not sure who was using the clubs, but I'll bet I know who wasn't watering the grass."

"You mean Robbie?" said Mr. Tee.

"I'm afraid so," replied Wendy.

"What do you mean I haven't been watering the grass?" demanded Robbie.

"For one thing, the sprinkler has been watering the front grass, not you," said Wendy.

"So what? I don't have to be holding the hose to water the grass," said Robbie. "I've been checking the sprinkler every few minutes."

"No, you haven't," said Wendy.

Why does Wendy think it was Robbie who used the golf clubs?

"It's hard to water the grass with a stopped-up hose," said Georgie.

"You didn't even know that had happened," said Peter. "If you had, you wouldn't have said you'd been watering the grass."

"Why don't we see how wet the grass is?" said Mr. Tee. Sure enough, the grass was almost dry.

Caught in his lie, Robbie confessed that he put the sprinkler on while he tried out the golf clubs.

"I'll pay for the broken club," Robbie said.

"Of course you will," said Mr. Tee. "And I'll have to think about whether I can let you work here any longer."

"Looks like Robbie's luck just ran out," said Georgie.

Solution
The Case of the Broken Golf Club

"How can you be sure of that, young lady?" asked Mr. Tee.

"Because he didn't know about Mr. Archwell's car being parked in the drive-way," said Wendy.

"So?" said Robbie. "He parked in the driveway. He must have come when I was in back."

"He was here for quite a while," said Wendy. "About twenty minutes."

"That doesn't mean I wasn't watering the grass," said Robbie.

"It wasn't just that his car was in the driveway, Robbie," said Polly.

"It's what the car did while it was here," said Mortimer mysteriously.

"So what did it do?" shouted Robbie.

"One of its tires was sitting on your watering hose for about twenty minutes," said Samantha. "It stopped the flow of water."